Ink Slingers

By

Writers of India

Ink Slingers

Anthology Book: **Ink Slingers**

Published by: The Wordings
Palwal, Faridabad
Haryana-121102

Email: contact@thewordings.com
Instagram: @thewordings1
Facebook: @thewordings1
LinkedIn: The Wordings
Web: www.thewordings.com

The Wordings
"Reviving Literature in the era of technology."

Co-Authors

1. **Astha Khandelwal**

2. **Megha Shah**

3. **Nidhi Patel**

4. **Sampurna Dasgupta**

5. **Seema Kumari**

6. **Shefali Kohli**

7. **Swathi M**

8. **Toiyash Dhar**

9. **Urmila Chakraborty**

Astha Khandelwal

Astha Khandelwal daughter of Gouri and Ashok Khandelwal, belongs to Raipur Chhattisgarh is a teacher & writer who has written a lot of poems in books, and short stories, she has also written articles for many newspapers.

Unexpected friendship

There was a girl named Richa Agarwal, she had shifted to Jabalpur with her family from Kolkata and started her career as a teacher and pursued her studies, she had taken English literature as her subject in college. Richa was a shy girl who had zero sense of style but was friendly. In the first day of college she made a lot of friends, and was loved by all. Soon the college started and she loved going and spending time with the new group which had five-member. During her college life, she was not so interested in studies but she was interested I'm going to pubs, and drinking hooka though her brother used to stop her but she never listened. Soon she fell in love with a guy in her group and confessed her feelings but they turned it into a joke and made a joke out of her ragged her after which she left that group. And soon she was left all alone after the death of her mother, she focused on her studies and soon completed her B. A and M. A in English. She scored highest in her batch and became the student of the year. She published a lot of article and made quite good friend in M. A period. She had detached from boys, she neither trusted them nor trusted the feeling of love. Richa's life was not easy at all without her mother she was all alone her friends had even ditched her as she was not smart in every birthday where she expected something good to happen everything changed. She was left all alone on her birthday even though she had a one good friend Shruti who tried to make her life better. But still she was all alone corona period came and she was at home, it was 8 April 2020. That while strolling Instagram she accepted a guy named Abhishek Bora. She never used to talk to guys but his first message somewhat triggered a sense, his first message was "Is this a profile or a food menu". Soon they both started talking and it was in a fraction of a second that they started vibing nicely and connected to each other. Days passed they started video calling each other, telling the stories and experiences of life to each other. Abhishek was a kind of jolly nature guy he had a lot of girlfriends and loved doing time pass which irked Richa but she never said anything. Soon Abhishek came and met Richa and she was so comfortable with him that she had never experienced with anyone. After the meet a lot of things changed Abhishek's some friends created a misunderstanding between them due to which Richa blocked him but his brother cleared the air and rumors soon Abhishek was trapped in s trap by some girls and it was Richa who stood by him and his family and cleared the name and this is when their bonding became more strong. Though there were times when they fought as if it was an end to the growing friendship and the fault was mostly of Richa as she behaved like a child. But still, they gave each other chance and focused on making their bond strong. Both of their life changed completely and they became each other's support and focused on growing more and making their future bright while keeping their friendship and letting it pass through all ups and downs and seeing whether it lasts or not till the end.

Megha Shah

Megha Shah is a practicing doctor from a small town, Malegaon but with big dreams and aspirations. During, this lockdown, she found her passion for writing and arts back and since then, there is no turning back!

Unexpected turn of events

I was running late, incredibly late! The only thought in my mind being 'was it really necessary to sit around with those gossip mongers and talk like there is no tomorrow?' Now, here I am praying, that I don't miss the last train to my friend's wedding destination-Goa. After paying the cab driver extra for helping me catch the train, I run up the Dadar station to catch the train. But my luck was not on my side and the train took off when I was climbing the stairs to the Platform! Immediately, I checked my phone to look for another train, but found out this one was the last for the day or should I say night! Now, here I am stuck in the middle of the station trying to fix this situation. Deciding to wait and leave my friend a text saying,"I will take up the 5 am train." It was already 1 am and my home was far away, so waiting on the station for the next 4 hours seemed to be a reasonable option. To pass time, I opened the book that I originally planned to read aboard. Time passed and it was 2 am, and when I lifted my head from the book, I saw a group of men were walking towards my bench. Looking at them gave off creepy vibes to me! And I was forced to reconsider my decision of staying back on the station. I looked around and found a family waiting nearby, deciding to sit next to the family will be my best bait. I got up and took my belongings and began my way to the family. Unfortunately, the men as well started following me, making me scared for my life! They knew that I was running away from them, and that gave them a kick, so they followed behind me. In all this chaos, I bumped into somebody and dropped the book in my hand. I bent down and started picking it up. On straightening, I turned to see the men and found that they had stopped. Relieved, I turned to look at my saviour, now this guy seemed to be familiar, so I dared to ask his name, he replied "Aditya Somani, May I know yours miss?" That name rang bells of familiarity in my head, but I was unable to point out the origin yet, so I answered, "Rhea Sharma" feeling grateful, I added, "You, literally saved my life Aditya, Thank you!" He seemed to be sort of shocked and looked me up and down, now I started feeling doubtful about my previous assumptions. I noticed him taking in my statement and looking behind my shoulder towards the men. This action of his, made me think 'is he involved with them', but suddenly he smiled, a full 1000 watt sight blinding smile and said, "Wow, Rhea you don't recognize me, do you? Let it be, I am Aditya, we were classmates back in school, in Nashik." Now, this put me in a frenzy to reopen my school memories, and I realised he was not lying and he actually was the ' Ever silent and observant Aditya Somani'. I gave him an equally blinding smile and asked, "What are you doing here at this time? Are you also coming for Pooja's wedding in Goa? And when did you start talking this much? I remember you were the silent guy in school." To this, he laughed out loudly, causing my cheeks to heat up in embarrassment and said, " Woah, the ever talkative Rhea, one question at a time please," and that made my pink cheeks turn red,"

Yes, you are right, I am here to catch a train for Pooja's wedding. I know, I missed it, so I was roaming around the station to passtime and catch the 5 am train, and here I bumped into you. And to answer your last question, I was a silent kid back then, but now I have become a social person, so the change." " Aditya, you have become unrecognizable, but I like the chatty version of yours more than the previous one. Now, since we both have missed our train, let's catchup, Shall we?" He said,"Sure." Sending a smirk in my direction, "Rhea, you are still the same person, I have known since school. So, I bet you must be talking with someone and lost track of time." That assumption of his, made me chuckle with embarrassment, and that was enough to prove his doubts. In return, I asked,"You must be busy with your business, to have lost track of time, am I right or right?" He laughed out loud and said, "Yes, you are right." After a few seconds he asked, "How do you know, I'm a businessman?". Flustered, I thought no point in hiding the truth, I said,"I always knew, you wanted to be a businessman." He was stunned and said, "I never knew you paid attention to me, in school!" Reddened from his response, I said,"I always did, Aditya, I have liked you since school days...". After a few moments of silence, my brain and mouth seemed to reconnect, and I quickly added," I think the late night is messing with my thoughts, I didn't meant that, I am sorry!!" Aditya caught a hold of my elbow, turned me around, analysed me, and said,"Well, I always have liked you, Rhea!!". I looked up at him, to see a cute pink shade on his cheeks, causing mine to turn redder. "Well then, I'm grateful to this night, Aditya, it finally connected us." "Yeah!" That's how, Rhea met Aditya, her hubby! And the night changed their lives for good!

Nidhi Patel

Coming from a loving small family, she is a budding writer who aims to show the world about feelings of oneself and of others through vibrant words. Her love for reading and writing, wants to make a name of her own.

Depth of beauty

'Finally it's over' I thought as we landed back to our land. The days of misery, loneliness, feeling breathless on those open fields, feeling hopeless, helpless, miserable, vulnerable came to an end. We were finally free, 'I' was finally free. We moved toward clearer skies, leaving those sand dunes behind, those dust still stings in my eyes. I feel the phantom pains of the injuries that i didn't even sustained. My head aches, my stomach is grumbling, my knee hurts but the scratch underneath my shirt, and over my arm is what scares me. It over, it's over, it's over ... I chant like a mantra. In all my life's mistakes, joining the army was my biggest regret. Leaving her behind is my biggest regret. This regret has left me awake on those silent nights, and kept me scared in those loud mornings. Part of me hoped that you have stayed, other part wished, that you would have moved on. You didn't deserve this. I didn't deserve you, your love, your patience, your sacrifice, which you didn't asked to face. You happily accepted the consequences of my decision. We didn't had any strings attached, no commitments in the face of law. You still told me, that you would be waiting for me, promised me... I wish you wouldn't have. Cause the man that has returned from the war is not the same who went there. The young guy you fell in love with is buried deep down in this shell filled with scars. You don't deserve this, my baggage. Emotional and physical. You don't deserve to carry the weight, I am bringing back. You don't deserve this. I don't deserve you. I wish, really do, that you are not waiting for me at the other side. I also wish that you do. I knew you never break your promises. That is that one thing I love and hate about you. You make sure one fulfills his or her promise. You are stubborn and stable, like an ocean. That light in your eyes is still the same, the glow on your face, scare away the dark thoughts, that smile now hold a little tinge of sadness but there is still a lot of joy behind it. I never thought those pain would fade. But one look at you and I again feel like twenty one. That young boy with million dreams and billion thoughts. One who had nothing but everything. He who was fearless, careless, reckless, seamless, even scar-less..... I can't bring you close to myself. I feel that my past will follow me all the way back here, and get hold of you. I don't want you to lose your smile, your shine, your beauty..... Your beauty is not what others see on the surface, it's was I saw beneath it. You bring best out of people, you push them out of there comfort, but you also bring comfort with your presence. You fix things, solve problems with ease... But i don't want to be that blotch on your life that you can't fix, that you can't solve, that mystery that you can't unveil... I fear you will see those scars. These scary red marks over my arms, covering my conscience. I had all good reasons to do it and hundreds of why I shouldn't have. Watching my friends, no Comrade, getting hurt, shot, die. Feeling hopeless, helpless, miserable, and vulnerable. I think it's survival guilt. I think all those scars was ne compensating their pain, for what I should have I also suffered.I felt,I wished to end it for once and for all, but I couldn't imagine you waiting only for me to return in a body bag. I wanted to prove you that I was still the same boy you loved, but am I still the same... I can't show you this body, filled with bruises and burns, cuts and scraps, harm brought by others and myself. I am no longer your hansome prince you fell in love with. I am no longer that flawless hero you saw me as. I am now a shell of pain and regrets. Those abs have now shrunken to probing ribs, those wavy hair is now matted with sweat and blood, and those bright blues ocean eyes now hold those empty sand dunes. I am no longer beautiful. I am just scars that are left behind. But it was you, for whom that I never crossed the line, for who I always stopped before I bleed out. It was you that I bandaged those broken bones, It was you, and your beauty I wanted to see one last time, that pushed me to stay. To stay with you. And now you have seen those scars. You have seen how flawed, distorted, weak, how much of a coward I am. How selfish I am to think that these red lines can make up for what my friends at field suffered, for what you at home went through. How I don't deserve to be honoured for my work at war, how there shouldn't have been a party to celebrate my return. How I have been anything but fearless out there.how I brought respect to my town and proud to my family. How selfish I am to take credit for all this, when I am nothing but a scared soul. But you again look at me with those adoring eyes. Make me belive as if I have hung up all the stars and moon.

You hold my hand, look at those lines of regret, tracing them with your fingers, feeling those unhealed ridges and bumps. You hold my hand, tangle your fingers with mine. You bring that fist towards your soft lips and kiss those pains away like I am a baby with a scrapped knee. It worked, I laugh internally, how actually kissing out the boo boo, ease out the pain. You lift your head up. Your red tear filled, matches my blood shot eyes. "These are not scars, but those beautiful lines that tell me how hard you fought, not with enemies but with yourself, to come back to me, to respect your friends, to leave a mark of your friendship, that you will never forget. These are now part of yours and i love them, because I didn't fall for that handsome boy in class but for your beauty in depth. "

FIRST IMPRESSION

She stumbles upon the cafe, twenty minutes late, hair are all touseled, shoe laces untied, a twig with a leaf hanging

From her head and i can't see a purse or pockets on her summer dress, definitely no wallet to share the bill. Aggh this blind date has started with a disaster itself. Maybe if I ignore her, she won't know I am Mr.Sweetguy29.

Yupp that would be best... Ohh she is looking around the cafe, hide behind the menu, shit waiter didn't gave me a menu... She is looking, what do i do, what do i do... Yeah, phone, Yupp. Act busy act busy.... Oh great she took another empty seat near window... Oh she is waiting for me... I will also. Let her wait for twenty minutes, no... I was gonna ditch the date. Yaa... Maybe wait for twenty minutes max. Just see how long she stays...does I waited pretty long...

It's been ten minutes, till now she has been quite attentive to street outside.... Ohhh the waiter looks infuriated, I think she will leave now... What!! Why is she ordering if she can't pay for it... God.... Oh that dress had a pocket... Hmmm innovative.... So possibly she would also have some cash on her....

Ok so mine coffee and cake are done and so are the twenty minutes wait.... Maybe I wait a few minutes.... Just to see what she does..., she haven't touche her coffee though...

Her cappuccino is now a cold frappe... Maybe I should introduce myself... She is not bad looking and she is good nature too... Like she helped that granny out in the street... And dutifully came back to her seat... She has those soft brown eyed too, which in this afternoon sun is perfectly shining is all the right colors. And those hairs look fluffy too, I can imagine, she definitely used those fruity smell shampoos and stuff... Maybe she like those kind of hampers..... Nope stop it. Mind, before you go too far... You are ditching this date... Don't fantasise about gifting options for the one you stood up.... Or maybe I can meet her... And don't stood her up... Oh god that would be a terrible first impression... What she would think, he was sitting here all along and didn't came to meet me.... A slap would be definate.... Maybe I won't tell her I am her blind date... Just say maybe I saw you here sitting alone, may I join you... Maybe shared the story how our dates ditched us, swear some words toward me, of how dare I ditched such a beautiful date... I would be like those romantic stories online.... Than maybe in few years during our marriage I can tell her, or tell our kids,... How I met your mother.... Okkk too far ahead, come back comeback...

Okk you can do it John... Go. Introduce yourself. Buy her a coffee, maybe lunch too if coffee went well.... Worst she can say, she is loyal to Mr sweetguy29 and reject me, and I can go back to my apartment and cry my lonely self to sleep for losing such a brilliant opportunity and a beautiful girl over first impression.. Ok.. Now or never..

"Hello excuse me.... Are you sweetguy29... "So here, standing in front of me is this beautiful lady, red summer dress, with perfectly matching handbag and heals, damn, even her phone cover matches her dress. Her hair is set is a perfect clumsy bun... Few stands dangling at the side of her face... Her perfect white's totaly coordinate with her ocean blue eyes...and her smile completes the look....

I keep on staring at her till

"Excuse me... Are you sweetguy29? Are you also here on a blind date... I guess by the shirt, totally matches your m.o.. I am so sorry I got late... Like soo late, but car's tire got flat and I had to call and get it towed and I tried texting you, telling I might be late, but you weren't replying so I tried to come as fast as I can... Hope you forgive me...

The world blured around me, I literally can't hear a single word out of her mouth.. . As my vision travelled to the girl sitting by the window and first time in last one hour, we made eye contact... She hold it for a few second before turn back to her cold coffee...

"Umm sorry miss... You got the wrong person... I am not that sweetsaltyguy69"

"It sweetguy29"

"Yeah whatever... I am not that... Maybe the guy had left within few minutes of waiting.... You know how guys can be... So um excuse me"

I put a fifty dollar on the table and cleared the bill and went to the girl in summer dress... I try to tame down my hair and press down those invisible wrinkles on my pants... Just a deep breath..... And,

"Hy, umm I am John keener..if this seat is not occupied. Um can I buy you a coffee as yours is cold now... "

She smiled, she looks more beautiful from close,. "I don't see why you can't"

Ohh her voice, I feel literal butterflies in my stomach... I just hope, I make a good first impression.

Sampurna Dasgupta

Sampurna Dasgupta is a 9th Grader studying at La Martiniere for Girls School in Kolkata. She enjoys writing detective stories the most. Agatha Christie and J.K. Rowling are her favorite authors.

Midnight Murders

Brownish orange leaves clustered the diverging streets which were as cramped as the night sky with a million stars embedded in it. Strong beams of sunshine flew around like UV rays, piercing everyone's eyes. And there in that particular bus stop stood a six year old girl. "Amara," her dad calls her. Or perhaps I should say 'called'.

***

It's Wednesday. A rather rainy Wednesday. The petrichor outside seemed to overpower the aroma that her lasagna produced. The rain-soaked streets, rather deserted, seemed to take in all the pressure, all the temper that the rain gushed out on it, trampling and stomping on it. "Hello?" I ask trapping my phone between my ear and neck and swaying my saucepan with my blistered hand in such a way that the hungry fire licked the sides with swift laps. "Hello, is this Ms. Jordon, the private investigator?" "Uh ha, who's there?" I barked, trying my best to convey an indirect message of annoyance at being interrupted during supper. "Mr. Brown here, is it possible for you to come down to Northwood Street, 517?" Too bad he didn't get the hint. "My daughter's been murdered," he added as I let my saucepan down immediately, switching off the gas, but only in vain for I knew my burnt sausages would never return to the golden-brown ones I had imagined.

***

"Welcome," he greeted with a strained smile and rather preoccupied eyes. Scurrying into his small cottage, I flopped myself down on the armchair that his wife had kindly dragged out, without realizing that one of the legs was broken. "That's alright," I forced a laugh, standing up as I rubbed the part of my foot that I had managed to bruise. "Alright, introductions please!" I bellowed, taking out my pocket notebook that had merely a few pages left. "Jacob Brown, Amara's father; 38" "Violet Brown, Amara's elder sister, older by seven years; I'm 12" "Melanie Brown, Amara's mother, 36" "Julyn Pennyworth, Amara's aunt and Melanie's younger sister;" "Chloe Pennyworth, Amara's cousin, Julyn's daughter," "Very well, may I see Amara's body please?" I asked, standing up, putting pressure on my two arms. "Of course, the doctor is in her room too," I stood still for a second, my eyes fixed to that little body that lay crouched upon the cursed bed. "Strangled and stabbed," the doctor had confirmed. "Doctor, could you please give me an estimated time of the occurrence?" "About 3p.m." "Alright, where was everyone then?" "Library," Chloe had mumbled. "I was at my friend's place," Violet had grunted. "I had stopped by at the store to grab groceries," Melanie had sniffed. "I was playing bingo just outside town," Julyn had stuttered. "I had gone for a drink at a nearby bar," Jacob had muttered. "Who was in charge of Amara, then?" I asked raising my eyebrows. "The help," Jacob piped in and bellowed as a frail lady in her early twenties, auburn tresses tied up into a bun, collarbones prominent, eyes distraught and obviously suffering from eczema, trotted in. "Where were you?" I asked sharply. "Ma'am, I know nothing about it! I swear I don't! I wouldn't harm a fly!" she fretted with quivering lips as her grey eyes rounded up. "Answer to the point," I barked with a stern glance. "I was bringing back little Amara from school, you see. What a little bundle of joy that child was! I brought her back safely. She said she was going to change into her pajamas in her room, so I left. Right then, the bell rang and in came Mr. Brown. He was only in the washroom washing his hands when Mrs. Brown came in and asked where her daughter was. She scurried into her room and found her daughter dead on the floor. Mr. Brown and I scrambled off to see why Mrs. Brown was screaming like that. And oh, what a sight it was! What a dreadful sight it was! I shall never for…" "That will be enough. Thank you, Miss… Miss?" I cut her off. "Miss Austen," "Right, a few questions now. Mr. Brown could you please tell us the name of the bar you were at?" "Krester's Moon," "Very well, thank you. And Mrs. Brown, what about the grocery store that you were at?" "Northwood Hand," "And what about the library, Chloe?" "Hiraeth National Library," she had muttered.

*****

"Hello! Which book may I get you?" "Oh, no, thank you! I just came to well…er…" my voice trailed off. "Yes, ma'am?" the librarian asked me with utmost curiosity. "Could I have a look at the register?" I asked uncertainly as the librarian's eyes knitted and she mouthed 'That's strange' to herself.

"I mean, I would like to get a membership. I have to sign in the register tho, don't I?" As my hands signed my name in the allotted box, my eyes searched around, travelling from one box to another. "That's strange. Chloe's name doesn't seem to be here. Yet, she told me this is where she spent her afternoon,'

*****

At Krester's Moon, 4 p.m. "Good evening, Ma'am," a rather disinterested voice mumbled as the waiter dragged himself to me with a menu card. "Er, a glass of sherry, please," "Amateur," I heard him mutter under his breath. "Could I please get your name?" I asked with a forced smile as I leaned forward. "Mateo Lopez," "I say, was there a man here today? Rather stout, bald too, with thick-rimmed glasses and a small moustache," "Ah, you're talking about Jacob! I had a drink with that fellow, I did. He came in and said he asked for tequila and bought a shot for me too. Quiet surprising for I didn't know he knew me!" "I see," I replied taking a deep breath as I put my left leg over my right one. "Why do you ask?" "Oh nothing, nothing at all," "He was a nice fellow...kinder than I expected him to be," "Oh, did you know him?" "Oh, he..." *thud* Mateo Lopez collapsed right in front of me. "He's dead!" I muttered.

*****

"Hello?" "Inspector? It's Lillian here," "How's it going, Lil? I heard you have a new case," "Mhm, I need your help.

Can you get a post-mortem done by tonight?" "Post mortem? Why, don't tell me there's been another murder." "I'm afraid so, Inspector. I was at a bar— the one Amara's father had visited on the day of the murder. I was talking to this particular waiter. He collapsed all of a sudden." "Dead?" "Dead." "And you have a feeling these two murders might be connected," "You know how a strait connects two larger water bodies? This is like the string connecting the murderer and the victim,"

*****

"Oh, looks like anther new fellow will be joining our weekly bingo betting," I could hear a voice as I pushed the door, before realizing that the signboard said 'Pull" Reconciling myself with a nervous cough, I pulled the door this time and trotted in as all eyes stared at me. "Will you be joining us, child?" a rather friendly woman in her early seventies asked me as I flopped myself on the seat next to her. "Definitely," I smiled, trying my best to sound interested. "Do you happen to know a lady called Julyn Pennyworth?" I asked after about fifteen minutes into playing the game, trying my best to not get to the point immediately but at the same time, desperate to leave that place. "Julyn Pennyworth, you say? Now that you say it, I do know a Pennyworth- but she isn't a Julyn, you see.

Beautiful blonde hair, she does have. Quite a frequent comer. I see her almost every day. Why, is she a friend of yours?" "Oh, oh yes. But I haven't seen her in ages. Do tell me more about her!" "Comes from a wealthy family, so I don't know what she does here honestly. Mysterious fellow," "Are you sure it's not Julyn?" "Absolutely certain, my love. Jess or so it was. She changed her surname too, got married a couple of months back," "And what about her new surname?" "It was Loop, no wait, Lopez, I think. Ah yes, Lopez!" "Lopez?" "That's right," she nodded taking out a box of mints and chucking three into her mouth. "And are you sure that she was blonde?" "I'm confident," she continued, drowning herself in more mints. "Right. And what about her eye color?" "My child, do you think I stare deeply into everyone's eyes? But as far as I remember it, it was a lovely, faint shade of blue," she continued. "I see, and when did you last see her?" "Well, she didn't come for quite a long time after the 17th. She started coming a few days later again, looking rather strained. Lopez used to always be at the bingo before going to the bar. I heard they even married without telling their family!" "Do you know the date of their marriage?" "23rd April, if I'm not wrong," "But if you are looking for a Julyn, I suggest you go through the register," she continued. "Right, thank you very much!" Flipping through the pages frantically, my eyes swayed from one cruddy signature to another one. My eyes came to a halt at 'Jess Lopez' but Julyn Pennyworth's name just didn't seem to be here, "Ah, what's the last day when Jess had signed?"

I asked myself as my eyes shifted to another column. "17th July, that's about a month back. Her signature seemed to have changed from Pennyworth to Lopez on 23rd April," I muttered seeing all the dates afterwards having 'Lopez' taken the place of 'Pennyworth," "Strange how the visits have become so very rare after her marriage," I muttered to myself. "Well, she must have developed a rather busy life after marriage." Glancing up at the column which said 'date of birth' I muttered- "13th October. That's strange, she seems to share he same birthday as Julyn." "Anyway, I suppose it couldn't have been her since her eye color is brown and not blue. Besides, she has auburn hair while this Jess Lopez is said to have blonde hair," I muttered trotting outside. "Lopez, Jess Lopez and Mateo Lopez. Could there be some connection between them or is it all just a coincidence?"

*****

"Inspector!" I smiled rushing inside. "Ah, you're here, Lil? You wanted to inspect the rooms, didn't you?" "That's right," I nodded looking around at every one in the room. There was Julyn Pennyworth seated on the armchair beside the fireplace with her usual bitter expression. At the table was Melanie Brown, eyes visibly sore from crying. There was Jacob Brown standing by his wife and forcing a smile on seeing me. Then there was Chloe nibbling on her nail, looking very disturbed and Violet standing beside her with a book on her knee which she obviously wasn't reading, for it lay upside down.

"I would hold the book the other way round if I were you, Violet," I smiled as she hurriedly coughed and straightened her book, flustered. "I say, where is Miss Austen?" "I haven't seen her all day now that you say it!" Melanie exclaimed sitting up. "What was the last time anyone saw her?" I asked sharply, turning around. "She was with us till dinner. We went to bed after that and I don't think we've seen her after waking up," Jacob muttered looking around. "Where does she sleep? I'll like to check her room first." "Of course, follow me," Jacob replied rushing in front and scurrying out. "What on earth?" Jacob exclaimed as he swayed open the door. I stop rooted to my spot, my eyes fixed at Miss Austen's body that lay on the ground. She had been stabbed in her chest and dried-up blood settled on the ground and on her beige, georgette dress. "Is she…?" the Inspector's voice trailed off. "She's dead," I sighed, turning around. "No way," Jacob Brown gasped, his eyes nearly bulging out. "Not another death in this house! Wasn't one enough? One calamity after another strikes this cursed house!" Melanie Brown cried, clutching on to the nearby doorknob. "Mr. Brown, will you kindly take her to her room while I call the doctor? She's suffering from a panic attack, I presume." "Naturally," he replied, leading his wife outside. "Lillian, do you think the knife that was used to murder Amara was used to stab Miss Austen too?" "Obviously not, Inspector. The cuts made here are much wider. I'll have to inspect the rooms now." I continue taking off my hair-tie as my bun fell into a disorganized waterfall.

Ruffling my fingers through my hair I said "I'll start with Miss Austen's room; Violet, Chloe and Julyn, please be seated in Jacob and Melanie's room." "Right," the Inspector mumbled turning around as the others left. "A lot of things happening." "Quite a lot, Inspector. Three murders in the same house within the span of just two days!" I exclaimed, browsing through the shelves and rummaging through the drawers. "Aha!" "Now what?" the Inspector exclaimed, scurrying towards me. "A knife?" he continued. "A knife," I confirmed. "The knife that had been used to stab Amara, but not Miss Austen." "And a stack of notes. That's a whole lot more than what Miss Austen would get in an entire year, don't you think?"

*****

"Alright, Julyn's room now," I bellowed. "Here," she grumped showing me in. "Thank you. Please join Melanie and Jacob Brown now," "Quite boring, isn't it?" I asked as my eyes shifted from one wall to another once Julyn had left. "The walls are too… er, brown," the Inspector replied trying his best to agree with me despite finding the shade beautiful. "Anything interesting here?" "Not really," I replied softly. "I wonder if she's a stage actress. This room is just filled with the things an actor needs- wigs, extravagant costumes, tiaras that are unnecessarily large and contact lenses in every possible shade."

*****

"Chloe's room now," I announced swaying open the door. "Right," the Inspector bellowed.

"Anything, in particular, Lil?" he continued. "Come here once, won't you?" I asked, squinting as I picked up a knife from the drawer. "A knife?" "A knife," I confirmed. "The knife that had been used to stab Miss Austen," "And how can you say that?" "The blade is such that the wounds could not have been too deep. According to my deductions, two knives have been used to stab Miss Austen—one that doesn't cut too deep, and one that cuts very deep. The doctor said that the deeper wounds have been made first at around 1 a.m. and then the shallower ones have been made at around 2:15 a.m." "Do you think it's by the same person?" the Inspector asked raising his eyebrows. "It's too early to say," I laughed. "Why, look at this!" "Now what?" 'Her alarm clock seems to be set for 1 a.m. - that's when Miss Austen was first stabbed," "Is it Chloe then?" "That's not all, Inspector. Look at this bottle of perfume," I piped in, picking up a bottle from one of the shelves. "I haven't seen any perfume that is blue before, Lil," he muttered with his eyebrows knitted. "Exactly. Try smelling it," I urged as the Inspector reluctantly took a sniff. "Cyanide."

*****

"Jacob and Melanie's room now," I bellowed as they showed me in. "I say, what's this?" the Inspector asked in an amused sort of manner as I skipped towards him. "Injections?" I asked. "Looks like that, doesn't it?" the Inspector continued. "There seems to be white traces in here," I exclaimed snatching the injections. "Of some medicine perhaps?" the Inspector guessed.

"Let's look around first," I muttered again. "Who do you think it is? Chloe seems rather suspicious, doesn't she? The knife used to kill Miss Austen, and the cyanide were both found in her room," he muttered. "Stop talking," I muttered giving the Inspector a nudge. "Wha…" the Inspector's voice trailed off as he followed my gaze and saw the shadow that fell on the floor. "Someone's eavesdropping," he muttered. "Why, it's Violet!" I exclaimed raising my eyebrows as I swayed open the door much to the surprise of the twelve-year-old girl. "What do you think you're doing here, young lady?" I asked as I beckoned her to come in. "I… I came here to grab the clothes for laundry," she gulped. "Really? Very well then, you may take it and leave," I replied sternly. "Thank you," she mumbled and scurried in, grabbing Jacob's jeans. "Just a pair of jeans? I thought you wanted to do the entire laundry," the Inspector piped in. "Oh, this pair takes a long time to dry, you see," she muttered as she scurried off. "Strange, do you think she really was here for the laundry?" the Inspector asked once she left. "Of course not, but do let's visit the washing machine later," I smiled back. "Huh?" the Inspector asked, perplexed. "Jacob's pair of jeans—there's something about them," I explained. "Ask Melanie, Julyn and Jacob to come in now, won't you?" I requested, as my eyes fell on a painting. It was a 12 by 7-inch long picture of three girls in their twenties. Melanie, Julyn and a girl who looked identical to Julyn. Julyn stood with her auburn hair and brown eyes with her arm around the similar girl who had blonde hair and blue eyes.

Melanie stood on the right enveloping both the girls in a rather large bear hug. "Ah, you're here!" I exclaimed as they came in. "If I may ask, would one of you care to explain who this is?" I asked curiously pointing to the picture of the girl who looked similar to Julyn. Seeing everyone exchange glances, I continued. "That's Jess, am I right? Jess Lopez." Knitting her eyebrows, Julyn piped in-- "That's my twin sister, Jess, but she never married. Her surname was always Pennyworth, not Lopez." "Oh?" I asked. "But surely, that lady at the Bingo had mentioned that her surname was Lopez? And I had seen it in the register too," "I beg your pardon?" Melanie asked, rather confused. "Nothing, nothing. But do tell me what happened to Jess." "She passed away last month—23rd April," Julyn answered. "23rd April—that was the date when Jess's surname changed from 'Pennyworth' to 'Lopez'; she couldn't have married him after her death. That is absolutely ridiculous!" I muttered to myself. "She fell down the stairs, you see. She had a habit of sleep-walking," Jacob Brown explained. "I understand," I replied. "Now, if you three will excuse the Inspector and me, we have a particular corner of this house to visit.

*****

"Did you find it?" I asked as the Inspector craned his neck, taking out a pair of jeans. "You bet I did!" he exclaimed standing up. "There seems to be something here," he murmured, feeling the pockets. "A tiny bottle," I murmured curiously. "Ammonium dichromate, don't you think?" he asked. "The same poison that had been used to kill Amara," I sighed. "Amara hadn't been poisoned, Lil. She had been stabbed and strangled," "So it seems. But I had asked the doctor for a post-mortem," "And?" "Ammonium dichromate was found."

*****

"Why, look at this knife!" I exclaimed, walking past the kitchen. "It's just a kitchen knife, Lil," the Inspector huffed. "The kitchen knife that had been used to stab Miss Austen," "Huh? But didn't you say that the knife that we found in Chloe's room was used to stab her?" "I did, but I also mentioned that two knives had been used to stab Miss Austen—one longer, and the other shorter, but with a sharper edge,"

*****

Next day-- "Hello?" I groaned at being disturbed in the middle of a very pleasant sleep. "Miss Evans? It's me, Julyn. There has been an attempt to murder Melanie and Jacob has been murdered."

*****

"Inspector, you're here too!" I exclaimed, rushing in. Melanie sat on her bed, shaking. Scars had been drawn on her legs and a bullet had landed on a pillow beside her. "Three inches higher and it would have been the end of her," the Inspector huffed. "We all woke up to Melanie's scream. We all rushed in and saw her in this condition," Julyn explained putting her hand on her sister's shoulder to calm her down.

"Melanie? When did you wake up?" "This morning. I woke up and saw these. I didn't even notice the bullet. It was Violet who pointed it out,"

Melanie managed to say in between quivering breaths. "You mean you didn't wake up when the scars were drawn?" I asked. "Not at all," "That's strange. The sound of a bullet being fired is loud. And the pain caused by a knife is a lot, if I'm not wrong," I continued. "What about Jacob?" I asked uncertainly. "His body is in the balcony," Julyn replied. I rushed to the window and craned my neck to see the lifeless body stabbed. "We found this beside his body," the Inspector grumbled as he handed me a pistol wrapped in sheets. "A pistol?" I asked, amused. "Are these Melanie's?" the Inspector asked, looking at the injection-tubes which had white traces inside. "Mel's diabetic. These are her insulins," Julyn piped in. "Miss Evans?" "Yes, Chloe?" "I found this in my drawer," she replied handing me a knife. "This is the knife that had been used to cut Melanie's skin," I confirmed examining the cuts. "Chloe, are you sure you found the knife in your drawer or did you just put it there?"

*****

"Melanie, who do you think the murderer is?" I asked once everyone had left. "I never knew there was someone who hated Jacob and me so much. But I do know that Violet absolutely loathed Amara," she sniffed. "Violet? But why?" "Well, after Amara came along, we have never managed to pay Violet any attention, you see.

She hated us for the same reason, I assume. It could have been Miss Austen too, since she was the only one at home when Amara was murdered."

*****

"It's time I announce who the murderers are," I announced as everyone sat up straight. "You've cracked it already?" the Inspector asked, amazed. "Let's start with Mateo Lopez, shall we? A guy who I met at Krester's Moon—the same bar which Jacob Brown had visited on the day when the former died. The former—Mateo Lopez had been poisoned—the same poison that was found in Chloe's room. One of Chloe's bottles that contained perfumes had cyanide instead," "What nonsense is this!" Chloe raged. "It's true. Now, this cyanide had been implanted in Chloe's room by Jacob Brown!" I announced. "Miss Evans?" Melanie asked, shaken from all this. "It's true, Miss Brown. But you must let me finish," "Now, the motive. Why did he do so? It was because his wife—Melanie had been cheating on him with Mateo Lopez," I continued seeing the colour drain out from everyone's face. "Now, Amara wasn't actually Jacob's child. She was Melanie and Mateo's daughter. I saw the DNA test results on Jacob's table. On finding this out, Jacob killed Amara too. But Miss Austen saw him. He gave her a lot of money so that she wouldn't say a word, but later stabbed her at night. But Miss Austen was already dead. Melanie thought that it was Miss Austen who had killed Amara and thus, she killed her.

But Amara had not only been stabbed by Jacob and Melanie, but she had also been poisoned by Julyn as she knew about the DNA test. Julyn had also mixed cyanide into Amara's breakfast to get back at Melanie. Violet knew that Jacob had murdered Mateo Lopez by dissolving ammonium chloride into the latter's drink. Thus, she had pretended to get the laundry, just to get the bottle out of our sight. Julyn was in love with Mateo too, but Mateo was originally Jess's man. So, she killed Jess. Julyn is an actress. I saw a blonde wig and contact lenses. She dressed up as Jess and pretended to be Jess and ended up marrying Mateo Lopez after killing Jess. Julyn dissolved sleeping pills in Melanie's insulin and cut her legs at night. She saw Jacob at the window with a bullet. She killed him immediately in fright. She shot two bullets—one nearly reaching Melanie, and the other one landing on Jacob."

Breathe

Shutting my eyes isn't helping,

It's getting harder to breathe.

Taking a break isn't helping,

My lungs might go on a permanent break.

I travelled to Stoneybrook, the narrow lanes and sunshine warming my withering lungs.

I knew it could be my last trip.

It would be something I would remember, if I had time to remember.

I did not know if I had any time in my life left since I knew the end was nearing.

But no time would ever be enough.

I breathe, nearly suffocating, feeling my lungs closing in and my gasps getting heavier.

I breathe, the sound of the machines discouraging me.

I breathe, all the tubes prickling my wrist.

But I breathe.

"You'll be fine," someone from the crowd says.

I can't make out who.

"Breathe. Just breathe," someone else says.

That's all I've been doing. Breathing. Just striving through. Existing. Not living.

My cancer relapsed last month. I've been in the bed ever since, with tubes cutting through my wrists and machines telling people how I am because apparently, I'm too weak to.

All I can do for now is breathe.

And that's enough.

I remember the first time they told me I had been diagnosed with cancer with a 7 percent chance of survival. It had been a tough fight, but I had made it through— at least for a few years.

"Keep breathing," someone says.

I am breathing.

I close my eyes, knowing that I might not open them again.

It'll be a tough week.

***

I take deep breaths, my eyes shut. I stir, but my body is too weak. I try to raise my body but I'm too weak to.

So, I stay silent, on that wretched bed that I could die in.

I was dying.

I wish I could talk.

I wish I could go home.

I wish I could stay alive.

I wish I didn't have to die.

I wish I could breathe.

***

My eyes feel like they've been glued together. I try moving my arm but I don't think anyone notices. I hear murmurs but can't figure out what they are saying because I can't get my ears or brain to focus. All I can think about are my lungs. I try breathing but the defeat is stronger than the victory.

It's easier to give up and lose.

It's easier to die.

I could just die but I keep fighting.

I don't know why but something gets me to force my lungs to keep going.

I force myself to run another mile.

I fore myself to reach the finishing line.

But I miss it by an inch.

I'm almost there.

"She's awake," someone says.

I feel a prickling sensation as the pipes are meticulously pulled out of my wrist.

"You can take her home," I hear the doctor's voice.

I'm alive.

I breathe, staggering, heavy breaths.

I know I'll breathe— at least for now.

And that's more than what I ever dreamt of.

Seema Kumari

Seema is a student of law in Bokaro steel City. She use to write mostly on YourQuote app and she is has published her book in Hindi poetry shuruat. She is a determined girl. She gives all the credits for her writing to her friend Shalini and Neha.

तस्वीर

तस्वीर...।। (तस्वीर हमें बहुत कुछ देती है वो बचपन की यादें, वो डाँट बड़ों की, रोने हसने वाले सारे पल की धुंधली यादों को जैसे ताजा कर देती है, और खुद से मिल जाने का मोका भी दे देती है।) एक लड़की जो अपना सबकुछ पीछे छोड़ कर एक नए घर नए महोल में जाती है, बस इतना ही तो चाहती है की उसे एक खुशहाल जीवन मिले, यही तो समृद्धि भी चाहती थी। समृद्धि एक 28 साल की लड़की 3 साल पहले विवाह करके नए सहर नए घर और एक नए परिवार मे आई थी, बहुत खुश थी की उसे एक बहुत खूबसूरत परिवार मिल है जो समझेंगे उसे उसके सपनों को भी और उसका साथ देंगे और वो भी सबका बेटी बनकर खयाल रखेगी। तो एक साधारण परिवार की समृद्धि अपने बड़े बड़े खाब को लेकर नए घर मे आ गई, उसका सपना था की वो अपने परिवार में बोझ की तरह नहीं बल्कि कुछ मदद करने वाली बराबर की मेम्बर रहे, पर पहले पहले साल परिवार में रमने में और खुशियों में वो इतना खोई रही की उसे समय ही नहीं मिल अपने बारे मे सोचने का, और वो सोचती कैसे सबकुछ मिल गया था उसे एक अच्छा परिवार एक खुशहाल घर प्यार करने वाला जीवन साथी पर क्या इतना ही काफी होने वाला था?? बस ये सवाल वो खुद से करना भूल रही थी, अक्सर अपनी अलमारी खोलकर देखती तो उसको अपनी किताबें दिखती जिसमे उसके खाब थे आईएएस की पढ़ाई करने के, पर फिर किचन से आवाज आजती और वो किचन की ओर निकल जाती पर एक दिन तो ये सब सामने आने वाला ही था जब वो अपने

साथ वक्त बिताने वाली थी, वो वक्त आया 3 साल बाद जब परिवार संभालते संभालते उसने तस्वीर का वो पुराना फोटो एलबम खोल अपनी अलमारी साफ करते वक्त जिसमे वो थी और उसके खाब थे 26 जनवरी को जो उसने अपने पिता जी से जिद करके एक दफा यूनिफॉर्म खरीदवाया था वर्दी क्यूँ की वो देश के लिए कुछ करना चाहती थी, एक तस्वीर दिखी उसको जिसमे उसके पिता जी उससे पढ़ा रहे थे और उसे याद आ गया अपने पिता जी का सपना की एक दिन मेरी बेटी मेरा नाम रोशन करेगी जरूर... यही तो पिता का सपना होता है,अपने बच्चों को कुछ करते देखना खुश देखना तो क्या समृद्धि खुश नहीं थी... ऐसा नहीं था ये सवाल उसने खुद से किया तो उसने जवाब पाया की खुश तो वो थी बस वो सबकी खुशी में खुश थी अपने लिए उसको वक्त ही नहीं मिला जिसके लिए वो खुश हो, "तो आज तस्वीर का ये सिलसिला लंबा चलने वाला था क्यूँ की समृद्धि को थोड़ा खुद के लिए मुसकुराना था यादों में से खुद को ढूंढ के लाना था"। तस्वीरों में आगे बढ़ती गई तो उसे नजर परि अपनी उस तस्वीर की जिसमे उसने अपने कॉलेज में मेडल जीत था अपने विचार के वजह से और उससे याद आया की उसके शिक्षक कहते थे "समृद्धि बहुत काबिल है,अपने लिए कुछ बहुत अच्छा करेगी, हमें उम्मीद है", समृद्धि को वो तस्वीर भी दिखी जिसमे वो अपने दोस्तों के साथ मस्ती कर रही थी और याद आया उसे की कैसे उसके दोस्त उसे मैडम सहीब कलेक्टर सहीब ही कहा करते थे और वो हस पड़ी और आँख की उसकी जरा नम हो गई..। तस्वीरों में उसे अगली तस्वीर मिली अपनी सगाई की और याद आ गया उसे वो पल जब उसने अपने जीवन साथी को पाया

था और वो वादा जो दोनों ए एक दूसरे को किया था की "हम दोनों एक दूसरे के सपनों की उड़ान बनेगे, कोशिश करेंगे एक साथ मिलकर आगे बढ़ेंगे"।। समृद्धि तस्वीर देखकर खुश तो हुई पर थोरी सी खुद से जैसे खफा हो गई क्यूँ की वो खुद ही खुद को भूली थी उसने ही पहले खुद के लिए कोशिश नहीं की तो कोई और उसके लिए क्या करता, और फिर थोड़ी खफा दूसरों से भी हुई की उन्होंने नहीं कोशिश की उसको आगे बढ़ने को कहने की अगर वो भूल रही थी तो खुद को याद दिलाने की। तो खुशियाओं तो थी ही सब कुछ था एक खुशहाल परिवार था पर तस्वीरों के इस सफर से समृद्धि 3 साल बाद आज खुद से मिली थी, और मिलकर मयूष सी हो गई थी, क्यूँ की 3 साल बाद खुद से मिली थी की उसके भी कुछ सपने थे उसकी उम्मीदें थे, हाँ वो मानती है उसके पास सबकुछ था पर वो खुद के पास जैसे नहीं थी, तो उसने जब अपनी आखिरी तस्वीर पलटी और खुद की किताबों पर से वो धूल हटाई और उन्हे अलमारी से निकाल मेज पर रखा और खुद से एक वादा किया वो अपनी कोशिश फिर से शुरू करेगी, क्यूँ की एक और तस्वीर उसे इस एलबम के लिए चाहिए थी, जिसमे वो अपने आईएएस के के सपने को पूरा कर चुकी हो और वो खुद से मिल चुकी हो और अपने अधूरे फोटो एलबम को ऐसे पूरा करेगी, समृद्धि ने कुछ ऐसा आज ठान लिया था। और किचन से फिर एक आवाज आई वो किचन की तरफ मुसकुराते हुए तो गई पर इसबर खुद को साथ लेकर गई, उन किताबों को देखकर मुसकृयाते हुए गई, अब भी देर नहीं हुई ये कहते हुए गई, जैसे तस्वीरों के जरिए ही वो खुद से मिल गई। यादें और उनसे जूरी तस्वीर असर हमे खोया हुआ बहुत कुछ

लौट देती है, तस्वीर और उनसे जूरी यादें इसिलए बहुत कीमती होती है, और इसी लिए अगर खुद से मिलन हो तो कभी अपने अलमारी में पड़े उस पुराने फोटो एलबम को निकालिए जरूर।

दस्तक....एक तरफा प्यार से सच्ची मोहब्बत तक

प्यार मासूम भी बहुत होता है और मासूम प्यार कैसे मुकमल होता है ये वही कहानी है, जब दो लोग एक दूसरे से प्यार में बस इसीलिए होते है क्यू की उन्हे होना होता है एक दूसरे की जरूरत नहीं आदत नही सिर्फ मोहब्बत होते है , कहते नही बस करते है सबकुछ और बेइंतहां प्यार भी बिना उसके मुकमल होने उम्मीद लगाए, इस कहानी से कुछ वही भाव मैंने कहने की कोशिश की है , और आशा है सबको इस कल्पना में भी अपनी अपनी सच्चाई मिलेगी जरूर ।

आज कॉलेज का पहला दिन था गर्मी का मौसम था वो चलते हुए आई , नीले रंग की सलवार कमीज माथे पर एक छोटी सी बिंदी और थोड़े बिखरे बिखरे थे उसके बाल और वो सामने आई और कहा "हेलो क्या आप मुझे बता सकते है फर्स्ट ईयर केमिस्ट्री की क्लास किधर है मेरा आज पहला दिन है मुझे पता नही है " और जिससे वो पूछ रही थी वो तो खोया हुआ था और लरखरती आवाज में उसने कहा आगे से लेफ्ट फर्स्ट रूम मैं भी फर्स्ट ईयर में ही हूं मेरा नाम सिद्धांत है, और उसने कहा शुक्रिया मेरा नाम श्रुति है (पहली नजर पर इश्क की दस्तक हो चुकी थी थोड़ी सी मोहब्बत तो हो ही चुकी थी पर अभी ये एक तरफा थी इसीलिए मुकमल थी एहसासों में, इससे इजाजत नहीं चाहिए थी उन्हें निहारने की उनके बिखरे बालों को देख मुस्कुराने की)। सिद्धांत ने कहा चलो मैं साथ ही चलता हूं ,

उसने कहा हां जरूर और दोनो साथ कदम बढ़ा कर चलने लगे ये जीवन का पहला दिन था जब कदम मिलाकर सिद्धांत और श्रुति चल रहे थे अब देखना ये था ये कदम बढ़ते है तो मंजिल कहा जाकर मिलती है इन्हे फिलहाल तो ये क्लास रूम तक आ गए और श्रुति पहली बेंच पर जाकर बैठी और सिद्धांत उसके पीछे वाली बेंच पर क्लास केमिस्ट्री की शुरू हुए और श्रुति के उड़ते बालों से केमिकल रिएक्शन सिद्धांत के दिलो दिमाग पर होने लगा सिद्धांत को पहले कभी ऐसा कुछ महसूस नहीं हुआ था वो खुश हो रहा था पर समझ नही पा रहा था ये खुशी हो क्यू रही है इतनी (दस्तक दिल में हो चुकी थी थोड़ी और मोहब्बत हो चुकी थी)।

क्लास खत्म हुए और सब एक दूसरे से hi hello करने लगे दोस्ती करने लगे और सिद्धांत और श्रुति भी थोड़ी बहुत बातें करने लगे कौन कहा से है, गांव शहर सब कुछ की जानकारी एक दूसरे को सब दे रहे थे और फिर हसी मजाक का सिलसिला शुरू होगया और श्रुति हस पड़ी एक बात पर और उसकी हसी की आवाज सिद्धांत की धड़कने बढ़ाने लगी पहला प्यार अपना असर कुछ ऐसे ही दिखाने लगा।

दिन बीते क्लासेज कैंटीन में बातें मिलना जुलना रोज कॉलेज में होने लगा और दोनों में अच्छी दोस्ती हो गई पर अभी सच्ची वाली नही हुई थी तो सिद्धांत श्रुति से उसका नंबर मांगने में हिचकिचाता था सोचता था बुरा मान गई और फिर नही बात किया उसने (मासूम प्यार) उनकी आवाज नही सुन पाएगा कल से अगर दिल की कह दी ये सोच के घबराता था।

फिर वैसे ही क्लासेज में आना जाना मिलना जुलना चलता रहा और फिर अचानक एक दिन श्रुति कॉलेज नही आई और सिद्धांत परेशान होगया उसकी आंखे चारो तरफ बस श्रुति को ढूंढ रही थी और श्रुति उसे जब नही दिखी तो वो बहुत कुछ सोचने लगा "ऐसा तो नहीं होता वो तो रोज आती थी उसे तो क्लासेज छोड़ना पसंद नही फिर क्या बात हो गई होगी वो ठीक होगी ना वो " खुद से सवाल कुछ ऐसे ही करने लगा (प्यार हो चुका था बेचैन मन अब हो चुका था फिक्र से चिंता तक का सफर तय होने वाला था सच्चा प्यार अब बहुत सताने वाला था)।

सिद्धांत कॉलेज के बाद घर आया और सोचता रहा फिर ये सोचकर सो गया की वो ज्यादा ही सोच रहा है सब ठीक ही होगा (प्यार में अक्सर हम अपने आप को सब ठीक होगा ये कह कर दिलासा दे देते है जब मेहबूब की खबर नही मिलती) ।

अगला दिन था कॉलेज जाने की जल्दी थी सिद्धांत को उसने मां से कहा आज नाश्ता नहीं करना कैंटीन में खा लूंगा और निकल पर अपनी साइकिल को हेलीकॉप्टर की स्पीड पर लेकर जैसे कॉलेज पहुंचते ही घुटनों पर बैठेगा श्रुति को कहेगा तुम कल नही आई और मुझे तुम्हारी बहुत याद आई ऐसा कुछ, (पागलपन की हदों तक पहुंच रहा था अब ये बेइंतहां मोहब्बत तक पहुंच रहा है)।

कॉलेज पहुंच कर फिर वही निराशा हुई आज भी श्रुति नही आई सिद्धांत निराश हुआ की उसने उसका नंबर क्यों नही मांगा था उससे उसकी खबर कैसे ले कोई दोस्त से पूछता कोई कुछ नही

कहता नंबर उसका उसने किसी से नहीं मांगा क्यू की वो खुद श्रुति से हक से उसका नंबर मांगना चाहता था तो अब सिद्धांत के पास कोई और चारा नही था इंतजार के इसी तरह दिन बीते रातें गुजरी सोचते हुए और श्रुति एक महीने तक कॉलेज नही आई और अब एग्जाम सर पर आगया सिद्धांत को भी लगा अब ये कहानी इतनी ही थी अब उससे पढ़ाई पर ध्यान देना है (नजर अंदाज करना भी प्यार करने का एक तरीका होता है जब कोई और उम्मीद नहीं होती तो ये भी दिल से छुपाकर इश्क करने का एक सलीका होता है) मन ही मन ये खयाल सिद्धांत के मन में आया एग्जाम देने तो वो आयेगी ही ना तब बात कर लेंगे।

सिद्धांत अब तक खुद से ये नही कह पाया था की वो प्यार मैं है क्यू की उससे ये समझ नही आया था पर अब आने वाला था ,घर की तरफ वो बढ़ रहा था और मन ही मन सोच रहा था की इतना फर्क उसके आने नही आने से क्यों पर रहा है उसके होने नही होने से क्यों पर रहा है और फिर अचानक उसकी वो हसी उससे याद आगे जिसपर वो भी मुस्कुराने लगा था, उसको याद था श्रुति ने जब उसे पहली दफा देखा था उसकी आंखों का काजल जो थोड़ा बिगड़ा था, उसे वो नीले सलवार कमीज में आते हुए ,कदम उसके साथ बढ़ते हुए क्लास रूम तक जाना और उसके बालों को बिखरते देख खोते जाना ये सब याद करके वो मुस्कुरा रहा था और उससे एहसास हुआ की वो तो प्यार मैं अपना सबकुछ भुला रहा था, या तक की घर भी वो दूसरे रास्ते में आगे बढ़ता जो जा रहा था (बुधु)।

अगले दिन जब वो कॉलेज पहुंचा तो उससे वही हसी सुनाई दी,

उसकी आंखों में एक चमक आ गई और वो ऐसे क्लास रूम में पहुंचा जैसे बस वही तो उसकी आज की मंजिल थी, और उससे श्रुति नजर आई लाल और पीले रंग की सलवार में माथे पर वही छोटी सी बिंदी और होंठों पर वही प्यारी सी हसी और सिद्धांत का दिल जोरो से धड़कने लगा और बस सच्चा प्यार हो ही गया मुकमल प्यार हो ही गया (अभी एक तरफा था पर मुकमल था क्यों की प्यार भी इसका था और करने का हक भी अब तक सिर्फ इसका था, पर अब ये प्यार और चाहेगा उससे भी प्यार हो ये भी चाहेगा पर सच्चा प्यार है उसके हां या ना से ये कम नही हो जायेगा)।

क्लास में सिद्धांत अंदर गया और फिर वो दोनो एक दूसरे से बात करते तभी क्लास शुरू हो गई क्लास खत्म हुए तो फिर श्रुति दोस्तो के साथ कैंटीन चली गई सिद्धांत कुछ बोल नहीं पा रहा था और वो सबके साथ बोले ही जा रही थी है रही थी बातें कर रही थी और ये चुप चाप ये सब बस देख रहा था , (आज सुकून मिला था दिल को तो दीदार करने की इज्जत थी आंखो को जैसे) उसके बाद श्रुति सिद्धांत के पास आई और कहा और तुम कहा खोए हो एग्जाम की तयारी में बहुत पढ़ रहे हो और सिद्धांत का वही हाल था जो गालिब ने कहा है (इश्क ने हमें निकमा कर दिया वरना आदमी हम भी काम के थे) सिद्धांत ने कहा हां थोड़ा बहुत बस और फिर ऐसे ही बात होने लगी वो पूछती रही ये बताता रहा और अपने दिल का हाल छुपाता रहा और क्लास खत्म हुई और दोनों साथ बाहर तक गए गेट तक पहुंचते पहुंचते कितनी दफा वो सोचता रहा की नंबर मांगे पर कुछ बोल ही नहीं पाया......और

शायद ऊपर वाले ने उसकी सुन ली और मदद कर दी और श्रुति ने ही कहा अपना नंबर दे दो मुझे नोट्स चाहिए होंगे इतने दिनो के एग्जाम है , और सिद्धांत इतना हरबारा गया जैसे किसी ने उसे उसकी फेवरेट ice cream दी हो जो तुरंत पिघल जाए तो तुरंत खा ले वो, वो अपना नंबर वैसे ही बोलने लगा और श्रुति ने कहा हंसते हुए " थोड़ा धीरे-धीरे बोलो आराम से मैं नंबर लिखकर ही घर जाऊंगी" (hihi)।

फिर दोनों अपने-अपने घर की तरफ चले गए और घर पहुंचते ही सिद्धांत को मैसेज आया "हेलो प्लीज नोट्स भेज देना श्रुति", और सिद्धांत जैसे खुशी से पागल हो गया की उसे श्रुति का नंबर मिल ही गया और अपने कमरे में नाचने लगा , फिर अपने आप को कंट्रोल करते हुए लिखा भेज दूंगा don't worry मैं हूं तो आपको कोई दिक्कत नही होगी, (flirt करने की कोशिश पर उतनी अच्छी नहीं थी ना)।

सिद्धांत ने फिर आगे लिखा "अच्छा ये बताओ थी कहा इतने दिनो तक तुम" श्रुति ने कहा " घर पर ही थी क्यों " सिद्धांत ने फिर कहा "मेरे कहने का मतलब है कॉलेज क्यू नही आई" उसने कहा "अरे बस यूं ही " सिद्धांत भी आगे कहने में थोड़ा हिचकिचाने लगा और समझ गया की अभी वो उसके प्यार में नही बस उसे प्यार हुआ है और वो रुक गया और फिर कहा " ठीक है जब बता पाओ तब ही कहना मैं नोट्स भेज दूंगा थोड़ी देर में",

श्रुति में ओके कहा और बात वही खत्म हो गई।

अगले दिन से असाइनमेंट्स और प्रैक्टिकल थे और मिलना नही

हो सकता था क्यों की दोनो के रोल नंबर के अनुसार दोनो का टाइम अलग था पर सिद्धांत के लिए अब श्रुति से कुछ भी अलग करने वाली बात अलग नहीं कर सकती थी, तो वो अपने टाइम से पहले उसके टाइम पर वहा पहुंच ही जाता था , श्रुति कहती थी तुम इतनी जल्दी क्यों आते हो, तो कहता था घर बैठे भी क्या करू तो कॉलेज आगया, उसकी ये बेवकूफियों वाली बातों से श्रुति हस देती थी इसीलिए वो ये बातें करता भी रहता था, उसकी मुस्कान देखने के लिए, उसकी हसी सुनने के लिए।

दिन बीत रहे थे रातें भी गुजर रही थी बातें हो रही थी दोनों में और गहरी दोस्ती भी और श्रुति को सिद्धांत की बेवकूफी भरी बात अच्छी लगने लगी थी वो रोज सुनने भी लगी थी उसकी बातें और फिर मौका आया तो सिद्धांत ने कहा मैसेज पर की "अब तो हम अच्छे दोस्त बन गए है अब तो बताओ कहा थी तुम इतने दिन" श्रुति ने भी आज कहा "बताऊंगी लंबी कहानी है" और सिद्धांत ने कहा कि "तुम लड़कियों की हर कहानी लंबी क्यों होती है, और बताऊंगी पर क्यू रुक जाती है", और श्रुति फिर हसने लगी और उसने कहा "तुम बहुत भोले हो और फनी भी" और सिद्धांत तो भई सातवे आसमान पर पहुंच गया अपनी तारीफ सुनकर और फिर श्रुति ने bye good night कह कर मैसेज भेजा और ये तो इधर खोए हुए थे आशिकी में।

एग्जाम भी इसी बात चीत के बीच आही गया और दोनो पढ़ाई में लग गए और दोनो एक दूसरे से कम बात करने लगे hi-hello बस और सिद्धांत कभी कभी कोशिश भी करता था तो डांट पड़ जाती थी मजनू को पढ़ाई करो अभी chit-chat बाद में, (एग्जाम

खत्म हुए और मोहब्बत का सिलसिला सुरु होने वाला था इसबर दोनो तरफ बराबर की आग लगने वाली थी जो एक तरफ तो कब से लगी ही हुई थी) ।

श्रुति ने खुद ही msg किया और सिद्धांत से कहा "एग्जाम खत्म हुए और मैं दे पाई इस बात से मैं बहुत खुश हूं" और सिद्धांत ने पूछा "मैं कुछ समझा नहीं" श्रुति ने कहा "कुछ टाइम पहले मैं जब कॉलेज नही आ रही थी तब मेरे घर में मेरी शादी करवाने की जल्दी चल रही थी पर फिर मेरी मां ने किसी तरह मेरी पढ़ाई खत्म करने के लिए सबको मनाया उसी सब वजह से मैं कॉलेज नही आ रही थी उस समय " और सिद्धांत चोक गया थोड़ा और फिर उसने कहा शादी ?? किस्से?? श्रुति ने मजाक करते हुए कहा लड़के से और सिद्धांत चिढ़ते हुए बोला " अरे ठीक से बताओ ना वरना मत बोलो" श्रुति ने कहा "तुम क्यों चिढ़ रहे हो, मेरी शादी हो रही थी चिढ़ तुम रहे हो"। सिद्धांत ने बड़े मासूम सा एक सवाल किया तो अब क्या ग्रेजुएशन के बाद होने वाली है लड़का पसंद कर लिया गया है तुम्हारे घर, और श्रुति हसते हुए फिर बोली "भोलू इतनी भी आगे बात नही बढ़ी थी, और फिर दोनो आज पहली बार एक दूसरे से एक दूसरे के दिल की जानने लगे थे , और श्रुति ने ही कहा "तुम्हे कुछ कहना तो नही " सिद्धांत बोला "कहना तो बहुत कुछ है पर कहे क्या क्या और कैसे , श्रुति बोली "सीधे सीधे बोलो क्या बात है" और सिद्धांत ने कहा "तुम मुझे अच्छी लगती हो" और श्रुति फिर बोली "वो तो मैं हूं ही"

सिद्धांत थोड़ा चिढ़ते हुए सच बोल ही पड़ा "मुझे तुमसे प्यार हो चुका है ", और श्रुति कहती है "मुझे भी भोलू" और सिद्धांत ये

मेसेज बार बार ध्यान से पढ़ने लगा और श्रुति ने कहा तुम मेरे लिए रोज प्रैक्टिकल के पहले कॉलेज आते थे मेरे घर पहुंचते ही मेरी खबर ले लेते हो की में ठीक से पहुंची की नही , और मुझे हसने के लिए कैसे बेकार से जोक्स तुम कहते रहते हो मुझे एहसास हो चुका था की तुम्हे मुझसे प्यार हो चुका है और फिर तुम्हारे भोलेपन पर मुझे भी एतबार हो ही गया मुझे भी तुमसे सच्चा प्यार हो ही गया "।

सिद्धांत रो पड़ा और श्रुति ने उसे कॉल किया और सिद्धांत को रोता सुन वो उससे और भी प्यार करने लगी और उसके भोलेपन पर और एतबार करने लगी और दोनो ने कॉल पर कुछ नही कहते हुए भी सबकुछ कह दिया प्यार अब एक तरफा नही मुकमल मोहब्बत में बदल चुका था दोनों को एक दूसरे की खामोशी पर भी एतबार हो ही गया था सच्चा प्यार अब दोनों को हो ही गया था।

कभी कभी चीजें बहुत आसान होती है, बातें बहुत आसान होती है, बस कह देने की बात होती है, और जो लोग हमे समझते है वो थोड़ा भी कह दो तो समझ जाते है, और अगर बात सच्चे प्यार की है तो सच्चा प्यार तो हर किसी को मिल ही जाना है बस उसकी दस्तक जब हो हो हमें पहचाना होगा और जिससे नही मिला तो समझ लेना तुम्हारे सच्चे इश्क का कही और ठिकाना है।

Shefali Kohli

Shefali Kohli is currently an undergraduate English Literature student at Sri Guru Tegh Bahadur College, Delhi University. Her research interests include Greek mythology, children's fiction, magical realism, modernism, and philosophical discourses.

The Mirrored Self

That afternoon, the one before Kiara's 20th birthday, her friend, a brunette, inquisitive girl, asked her, "Is this an old habit the way you talk to yourself that too in front of everyone?" Kiara raised her eyes from the table at which she had been staring for quite some time now, stupefied and perplexed. As soon as she opened her mouth, her voice had that hard but slightly croaky undertone that made her also question her own voice. She was dumbstruck when she heard the question as this thought never stuck to her mind. Since her mother and father died in a car accident, leaving her to survive alone in this unknown and unfamiliar world, she has had nobody to rely upon. It was just her, alone with her deeply embedded thoughts. She had to drop off from the university and take up a menial job at a restaurant as a waitress in order to make her ends meet. Therefore, she didn't know what to answer when confronted with that question. As far as she knew, this action of talking to herself was not a conscious one. She remembers talking to herself when she had no one to talk to, arguing and interrogating the only being that actually listened to her, her own self, and thenceforth she couldn't remember when that momentary comfort in her solitude became a habit. She looked at her friend, who was curiously waiting for Kiara's response, but Kiara held the words back and rolled them down on her tongue again and again till the time she let them out of her mouth. While discussing this with her friend, Kiara realized that the world was somewhat divided into two categories.

There is one type where there exists the world of living and dead, and then there is the other type, some force, that allows the intersection of the living and the dead. The latter one involves paranormal abilities in experiencing events, not in the sphere of the living, as well as premonitions and the ability to predict the future. However, Kiara never experienced any paranormal activity and never seen a ghost throughout her life. She wondered under which category her story belongs to and would she ever be able to classify her life that was far away from the normal daily life led by every adolescent, in such concrete categories or would she has to transcend these boundaries to make her own unique classifications, she did not know. She was considerably satisfied with her life, though she regretted dropping out of the university and compromising her dreams of someday becoming a professional chef with this menial job. It was night when she walked back to her home with ideas in her mind and questions about her existence. While walking alone in the long lonely street engulfed in complete darkness, she was still encapsulated in her thoughts. Suddenly, she noticed a yellow light coming from a wooden hut and a faint sound of music, as if coming from far beyond. Being a curious girl, she wanted to explore what was happening in that direction. As she went close to that sound, she noticed a small wooden cottage with a spacious lawn and a broken gate. However, as well as she remembered, there was not any wooden cottage the night before. Was she dreaming? She did not know. She went towards it without thinking of the consequences she might encounter.

Without thinking twice, she opened the broken gate and entered the cottage. Inside, the situation seemed normal. She did not feel anything odd, it was a well-lighted house, but she could still hear the music playing in faint rhythm. While she walked around the house, she shouted, "Is someone there?" No one replied. She went inside and saw a door that seemed dustier than most of the house. She could hear the wind howling the entire time and the windows banging together as if trying to coordinate with Kiara's heart thumping aloud. Was she afraid? She did not know. She just kept on moving as if her muscles were out of her control. She was being drawn to that direction, willingly or not. When she opened that mysterious door, she was petrified to see what was inside. It was completely dark with faint music playing, and a staircase led to the basement. While walking down the stairs with her torch, she thought she had seen something in the dark. She broke out in a sweat. Taking a firmer grip on the torch, she turned towards what she saw. And there SHE was. A mirror was placed oddly in the middle of the staircase. It was a long, full-length mirror. Relieved, though, she felt stupid of being scared by her own image. Feeling dumb, she glanced at herself in the mirror. After a couple of minutes, she noticed something odd. Her reflection in the mirror was not her. It looked exactly like her on the outside, but it was not her, it was another her, maybe her on the other side. She confronted someone familiar and unfamiliar at the same time. She knows this person she is looking at in the mirror but then why does she feel this horror gripping her heartbeat?

It is hard to express in words how she felt. One thing that was clear to Kiara, glancing at the mirror, is that this another her despised the real her or was the other one real? She did not know. The image of Kiara inside the mirror had a hatred for the one outside. The dreadful loathing between her two images was like an icecap floating in the gloomy deep sea, uncertain to break or mix with the sea yet unable to escape. She stood there, still and numb. Both of them kept staring at each other. There was silence all around. To her surprise, the reflection in the mirror tried to touch the face of Kiara outside the mirror. Her fingertips were cold and slowly reaching the throat of the one outside. She suddenly realized she was doing the same thing. She was bewildered. What was happening? Why is she losing her control over herself? Is she in another dimension of the universe? But no, that can't be the case as that happens in only movies. This is no movie. Everything is real, or at least FEELS real. However, how can there be two of them? She realized the Kiara inside the mirror was taking control of the existence of the one outside. Was it her old deep-rooted regrets she has had her entire life for dropping out of college? Or, those strangely unreal dreams she had about meeting her dead parents? She did not know. She was so confused to think rationally. Is there any other way to think? Is there any other way to comprehend this profoundly mysterious world where what seems real is perhaps unreal or the other way round? Wresting out her last ounce of strength, she roared out a loud growl.

She doesn't know what happened, but she felt a sudden and intense pain in her head that she was unable to bear. She continued to look into the mirror, dizzy and motionless, but to her surprise, she couldn't see the other Kiara inside the mirror. Confused, she fell unconscious to the ground. Perhaps the link between the reflection on the other side and her was broken with her growl. She did not know. She could not be certain what was reality or illusion. While being unconscious, she felt all her reality questioned all at once. In a state of frenzy, she raised the sharp wooden stick that she picked up on her way inside and smashed it into the mirror. The glass shattered, and with that, she saw her whole reality getting out of her control, crumbling down into nothingness. It was as if her past, present, and future blended into one, and she was afraid to even recognize which is what. To her horror, through the shattered glass, she saw her mother and father's blood-covered bodies reaching out for her help, but she couldn't reach them. She tried to, but their shivering hands slipped out of hers. Every night after this incident happened, she relived this event again and again throughout her life. She is still not able to comprehend what happened that night. Was there really any mirror? Or was it her consciousness laughing at her? She did not know. She wished she held those hands of her parents, but why could she not? Was it her destiny laughing at her or her strength? She did not know. That night she did not see a ghost. What she saw was HERSELF. Whenever she passes by a mirror, she still feels the bloody hands reaching out to her, calling her to the other side, but she could not hold them. She still feels the cold touch of those fingertips grasping her throat, trying to kill her. But, who was she? Was she from the other realm, or was she merged with that 'other' her becoming a completely different person altogether? Is that even possible in the human realm of existence? She did not know. The only thing she knows is she can never forgive herself for not holding those feeble, shivering hands of her parents. Henceforth, she will be forever stuck in this eternal cycle of trauma and regret. That night, she didn't lose only her parents but also herself. She couldn't find the zeal to continue living despite everything that happened that night. Unconsciously repressing those memories, she kept consciously repeating to herself, "I shall never sleep quietly again. How can I when my mind is filled with horrors that lurk ceaselessly behind me in time and space? I shall never escape this circle of suffering and guilt. Where shall I find any purpose for continue living this miserable existence? Why not end it for the last time?" These words echoed in her mind and heart every day she stepped out of the house, and she continued living her uncertain presence quietly in isolation for the next five years. She neither had a job to make her survival easy nor any hope to pursue her passion for cooking that she developed in her former years while standing and enquiring in the kitchen with her mother. She was living off the bare minimum food she had left and the little touch of hope she had left in herself. While walking to a grocery store to purchase a loaf of bread on another Sunday morning, she again encountered a mirror that was placed just outside the opposite shop. She tried to avoid her memories with the mirror earlier in her life and tried to walk without noticing it, but her attention was grabbed by her reflection in the mirror that, again, she could not resist. However, this time was different. This time she didn't see just herself in the mirror but herself as a minuscule part of the world she inhabits. She realised how small she was in front of the vastness of the world. Perhaps she is just a pawn in the more enormous chessboard that is the world, designed by a forever unknown entity. Or, she is just a puppet controlled by the hidden powers in the circus called the world. In this sublime vastness of the world and its possibilities, how can she be sure that she has no place in this world? That her existence isn't valuable? Even if it isn't, even if she doesn't have a purpose, can she not accept this fact that life is itself concealed to be revealed in its immense entirety? Perhaps she can still exist, despite her not knowing the purpose of her life or even the purposelessness of her existence. With these thoughts engulfing the deep compartments of her mind, her unconsciously repressed memories slowly started transgressing into consciousness. Maybe that night was a reminder for her to just let the past crumble down into nothingness and start living in the world with newfound awareness and acceptance. Looking straight into the mirror, in her eyes that shone like it had never before for the past five years, she found a regained enthusiasm for living. She was ready to press the restart button of this game called life.

Even if she is a mere puppet in the hands of an unknown entity, she felt empowered to take the strings in her own hands to control her actions and lead a life on her own terms, unassisted and emancipated, breaking the chains of the 'otherness' of her identity and reclaiming her own selfhood.

Swathi M

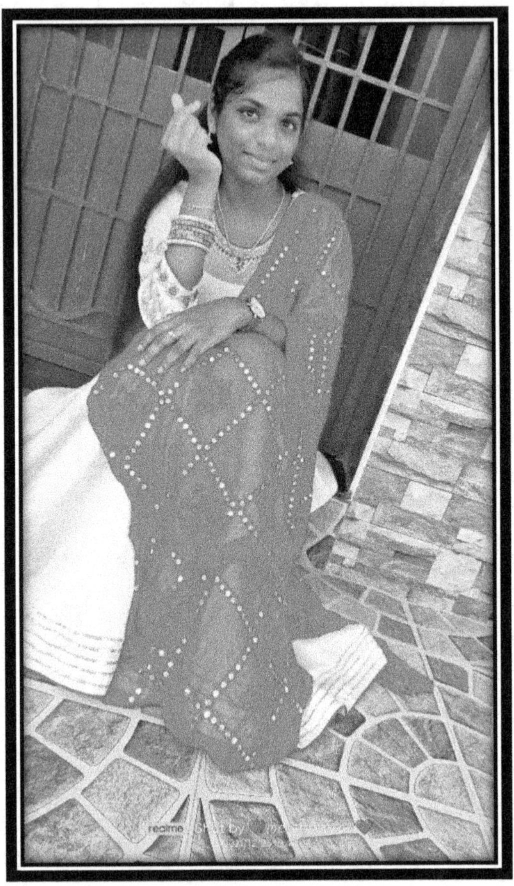

Swathi M is a PhD Research Scholar, Litterateur, writer and an anthologist. She is a strong believer of the universe and miracles who contemplates every moment and weaves poems and stories out of them.

Obstacles as a Stepping Stone

I have a recurring dream….. I'm on the verge of crossing the white line. I see another me on the other side of the line. I look the same as everybody else; the only variation is that I'm happy. I have cold feet every time I walk towards the line to cross it and turn around. Is it possible that I'll ever make it to the other side? Will I be able to pinpoint the source of my joy? My final day at the Juvenile Detention Center had come to an end. 3 years of my existence were spent in a room that looked like a gloomy box. The only people I knew there were a few buddies who snuck in and out through the cracks in the wall. I was given a job by the authorities. Reading has always been a passion of mine. As my mother used to tell me, this is a trait I inherited from my father. I never met my father, but I am glad that he instilled in me an interest in reading. My friends here have been Jane Eyre, Dorian Gray, Little Dorrit, and others. I owe them a debt of gratitude for holding me cozy on frigid evenings. Every day, I'd wake up to the same gloomy life. I wished to get out of here as soon as possible. Is it possible to get out of jail? No, I was well aware of the situation. I might have been in for things they thought were bad, but I knew deep down inside that I wasn't. As my release date approached, I received a letter with details on my new work and accommodations. I also had the privilege of attending fantastic courses on 'How to Deal with the Real World.' I didn't need workshops on how to deal with the outside world;

all I needed was a class on how to transform my life. Near the ancient railway station, there is a tiny bookstore. That's where I was supposed to start my job. My sleeping quarters were to be in the bookstore. "Mama, she's here," says the narrator. "Hello, it's lovely to meet you." "My name is Cilvin," was all I could think of. I wasn't anticipating this bookshop to be run by a woman in her late sixties. I've heard that elderly people are difficult to get along with. I'm not sure how long I'll be able to stay here. I was also curious as to how long it would be until she kicked me out. "Your chamber, Cilvin, is ahead." Keep your stuff, and I'll explain your responsibilities later. Thank you for your assistance, officers." I carried my belongings upstairs. The officer replied softly as if he didn't need me to hear what he was saying, but it was futile. "Please phone us if she acts strangely or if there is something wrong." They don't believe me, of course. In comparison to what I had at the centre, the accommodation was quite huge. Everything appeared to be in order. I could just see the subway station and, if I peered closely enough, the hills, from the arched doorway beside the bedside. That was the location of my residence. A little cottage nestled among those lovely green misty hills. I had completely forgotten about it. But I vowed myself that I would never return. The hills that had watched me grow from a little girl to a heretic were the same hills that had seen me become a sinner. After putting my clothes in the closet, I headed downstairs. I completed the task in less than five minutes. I just had a pair of bright blue denim jeans and three t-shirts with me.

That is all there is to it. "I've got dinner ready." "You must be starving." I was one of them. I ate all of the chicken curries she had made. It was the most delectable meal I'd had in a long time. Later, I scraped the bowl clean and drank the hot glass of milk. I was satisfied and satisfied. A two-story wooden home served as the shop. The shop was located on the ground floor. On the second level, there were two chambers and a kitchen with a small dining table that easily fit in the space. You had to cram yourselves into that cramped area. "Many thanks for the meal." "You don't have to thank me." "Did you enjoy it?" "Yes." "I'll take care of my business downstairs, and then we can discuss upstairs." After a while, she returned upstairs, beaming for some cause. She was incredibly active for her age. "How do you run this place by yourself?" I finally posed the question that was plaguing me for a long time. "I've always been quite rebellious," she replied with a smile. My parents were poor when I was little when I was younger than you. They were laborers who were paid daily. They laboured all hours of the day and night to nourish and educate the people. There are two sisters in my family. Both of them were married years ago and now reside in different cities. My sisters and I began working when we were fourteen years old. We used to live in a ghetto near the river. I'd hurry down and sat by the river after completing the steps and schoolwork. In my hands was always an old, ragged book. We couldn't even afford new garments, let alone books. Everything we wore, from our dresses to our underwear, was given to us by wealthy people who no longer needed it.

When my mother returned from work with a bag of old clothes and, if I was lucky, a storybook or two, I recall how happy we were. My parents instilled in me the importance of money and, more significantly, the importance of hard work. When I was younger, I made a pledge to myself that if I worked hard, got a good job, and saved enough money, I would one day buy a bookstore. I'm still here today, working at this small bookstore. I've always enjoyed working, and this bookstore is not only a source of income for me but also my entire universe." "Ah, I see."You did it," I responded. "I did," says the speaker. "You appear to be in a good mood; what happened?" When I noticed she was chanting and smiling, I inquired. "Today, an old customer and a beloved old buddy came to see me. It brought back memories of happier times. He was a good buddy of mine and came to see me frequently. He and his older son relocated to Australia a few years ago. After a long absence, he finally visited us." "Wow, that's fantastic." She retrieved a rusted coin from her wallet and dropped it on the desk. "He gave me an Australian souvenir." She smiled as she said, "A penny he found in a park." I couldn't figure out what was so amusing about a simply lost penny. I once discovered a misplaced sock. Is it appropriate for me to inform her about it? She would be ecstatic. "I'm sure you're wondering why I'm acting as if this coin came directly from the wallet of Australia's Prime Minister, eh?" I simply nodded. She was able to deduce half of what I was thinking. "Any gift from an old friend is a special gift," says the narrator.

When he first came into my shop, he noticed a penny on the floor. He approached me and informed me of the situation. I chuckled and told him he could keep it because it was his golden day. That was the start of our conversation. You see, it all began with a penny." "You have a knack for running the store." I shifted the focus. "Is that it?" She said, "Thank you." "May I inquire as to why you want me to work here?" It doesn't appear that you require assistance." "Recently, my advanced age has been getting in the way. The doctor believes I should take it easier and seek assistance at the shop. I went along with it. You'll assist me with client service and cleaning. At the end of the month, you will get compensated. "Is everything okay?" "Yes." "I..." "What exactly is it, Cilvin?" Don't be hesitant." "It's nothing," says the narrator. "Great night," she said. I returned to my room. Everything appeared to be in order. What more could I want than healthy food, a pleasant lady, and the opportunity to work in a library? I climbed into bed after changing into my nightgown. After three years in the juvenile center, the fragrance of clean linens and a headboard to lay my back were things I never expected to have. I was so tired from all of the traveling and settling in that I fell asleep almost immediately. The identical dream occurred to me once more. But this time, on the opposite side, I could see the old lady standing with me. We were quite pleased. A loud bang from the business downstairs jolted me awake. I dashed down the stairs as quickly as I could to see whether she was okay. "I apologize for waking you up so early in the morning.

I was cleaning the upper shelf when it all went to hell. "I should have been more cautious," she said, her gaze falling on the strewn mess on the floor. She began to gather them. I gently grabbed the books from her and assured her that I would take care of them. She praised me and invited me to breakfast after I was finished. "Does this happen all the time?" While selecting up a Daphne De Maurier collection, I wondered. After putting the books back in their proper places, I went into the kitchen. She had breakfast ready for us both on the table. Everything was beautifully set out, and the food on the table looked delectable. For some reason, I had tears in my eyes, which I wiped clean before they could flow down my cheeks. For a few minutes, I just sat and surveyed the breakfast table. I couldn't recall the last time I had a nice breakfast served to me at such a table. Have I ever? I tried my head for a bit but couldn't recall anything. "It's not a gazing contest," she explained, "and even if it were, I'm sure the food would have won." "Why me?" you might wonder. In hushed tones, I inquired. "Well, I didn't want to eat breakfast by myself, and I figured you'd be hungry, so I made some for both of us." "No. Why did you decide to hire me? You already know where I was before I came here. When you could have employed someone else, why did you say yes to hiring me? Or do you have no idea what I've done? I wasn't planning on committing petty theft." She opened her mouth to say something, but I was too caught up in my emotions to respond. "Three years ago, I murdered my stepfather in order to avenge the death of my poor mother.

I put an end to his continual squabbling and harsh behavior toward us. I defeated the demon that had enslaved us. Every day, I witnessed my mother pleading for nothing, and her injuries were getting worse each day. When I saw her lying in a red pool with her dear naive eyes wide open, I knew I couldn't handle it any longer. She seemed to be waiting to see me for the last time before she departed. I wish I was at home at the time. I hope so. After everything was finished, I set fire to the house. I couldn't stand looking at it. Did you have any idea what was going on? I am untrustworthy in the eyes of society. I don't expect you to have any faith in me either. I guess I'm a hopeless case." "Do you want to bury your previous six feet and go on?" Nothing came out of my mouth. "Isn't it true that you desire to transform your life?" You say you want to turn a new leaf, and I believe you will." "How can you have such faith in me?" "I'm going to take a chance." They told me about your time in the detention institution, which lasted three years. While you were there, you never displayed any violent tendencies. By reading literature, you found comfort in the words of others. Books are more than just stories about real or Helenginary people; they are a portal to another world. Sometimes books become our leader and show us the route in life, other times they make us cry because of the tragic figures, and still other times they make us laugh till we cry. Our silent but not so quiet companions are books. When you were younger, you did something. Why should you bear the load for the rest of your life? When you killed him, you were enraged.

But you must recognize that irrational emotions should never rule our lives. We must learn from mistakes and resolve to make positive changes in our lives. On one side of the river is the beginning of life, and on the other side of the river is death. There are stepping stones in between that must be carefully crossed. You must not give up even if you fall. Return to the top of the hill to finish the path in front of you. I'm not going to ask if you repent it, but would you like to return to the pebble and cross the river?" I took a look outside at the lovely Irises blossoming in her yard. I believe Iris flowers are a symbol of hope, according to something I read elsewhere. Tears streamed running down my face. This time, I let them run their course. I wanted to go away from the gloomy, awful life that had been haunting me for so many nights. I desired to be rid of the agony that had been holding me back. "Yes." She gave me a hug. That was something I really needed at the time. I rediscovered my lost self-assurance and determination to live. It has been ten years since she died. She entrusted the property to me. I began an 'Iris gives hope' book club a few years ago, and it has helped me tremendously with my isolation. I would have missed out on the great opportunities that life gave if I hadn't stayed on the stepping stones. As the saying goes, the options are endless. I'm pleased I didn't give in to my feelings of shame and grief. I'll confess that progress was slow, but I was pleased with myself as I took each stride forward. She gave me a new life with her warmth and wise remarks. Because of her, I was finally able to cross the white line.

Toiyash Dhar

Toiyash is a writer, enthusiast, learner, and excited for life's journey. A strong believer a pen can change the world.

Another Sunday

"Ohh... That felt good. I just don't know what just instant relief to morning aches is in this coffee... Especially the "Sunday coffee" just hits different. But I'll have to find a way out of these daily body aches. After all 46 is not that of age but feels like old age has started to hit." Oh, by the way, I didn't introduce myself. I am Peter Fernandez, PO at SBI Parel branch. Nothing too exciting in life, daily 9 to 5 job, rare holidays, and a pile of bank file works pending. But Sundays are different. Every Sunday gives me the hope to travel my 9 to 5 boredom. Coz today I meet my wife Jenny and my son Chris. Okay, enough talking now I'll have to go get a shower. There's really no fixed time for water and that to lack of rainfall even made it worse. Jennifer Fernandez... My Jenny, the purest soul I have ever seen. I didn't believe in love at first sight but after seeing her for the very first time I literally experienced it. The moment will always be special to me in fact the tiny moments I spend with her bring all my work stress out of my mind. Her blue eyes and bun hair made the best combination in the world. I call her eyes "Eyes of Heaven" and her face would go red. My Jenny... 'Trringg...trringg...' My old BlackBerry received a message 'Where are you, Peter? Chris is hungry and you are already half an hour late. Be on time at least today. Chris said he will not order until you arrive. Please come quickly. Bye Honey.' Yeah... Jenny's voice is just a pure melody.

I don't want to be late. After all we middle class need a month's saving to get into a good restaurant and I would not want to ruin that. Whhoo... Nowadays taxis are really hard to find especially when you are late. Two years after marriage we were blessed with a lovely God's gift. Chris, a child every parent would wish for. He had his mother's look. Eyes, nose, lips resembled his mother, but the hairs were mine. He is now 10. He plays football quite well. But the hard point is I don't get much time to spend with him. But today Chris will be happy as he really wanted to go to "The Aurora" and most importantly I got a day off the daily hassle. Ooof... This Mumbai traffic never takes a day off. The traffic police drenched in sweat trying to make way for the ambulance. The vendors are using the time best for selling their items. The cars honking each other for no reason at all. Typical Mumbai at its best. (Knock knock) Someone knocked the taxi window. 'Sahab... Fresh Gulaab. Only Rs 30' said a boy, mere 8 to 10 years trying to sell flowers at every car at the spot. I wanted to say no but couldn't. Didn't want to drop the expectation of the kid. 'Give me a piece'. 'What's your name? 'I asked while searching for the money in pocket. 'Raju.' His eyes searching for his next customer. Meanwhile a deep voice came 'Ayy... Raju. 'I looked through the window. A tall stout man standing with a bag. Raju raced in between the cars. Lost him in a glimpse. Suddenly, my eyes went to a group of kids in the roadside counting some money. Raju was also in that group. They were standing in the shade of a washed off banner.

The banner said "STOP CHILD LABOUR. EDUCATE CHILD, EDUCATE FUTURE." I couldn't help but smile. Finally, after overcoming the stubborn traffic I reached..."CATHOLIC CHRISTIAN GRAVEYARD". (Three years ago) 'Mamma when will Papa come' asked Chris. His eyes were glued to the next table's order. 'You know your Papa, always late but don't worry beta he's on the way' Jennifer said looking for Peter in the doorway. Chris's happy face had faded as his hunger took over him and there was still no sign of Peter. Jennifer sent a message to Peter 'Where are you, Peter? Chris is hungry and you are already half an hour late. Be on time at least today. Chris said he will not order until you arrive. Please come quickly. Bye Honey.' Jennifer called the waiter and told him to bring a plate of sandwiches to calm Chris a bit. Chris loves sandwiches. 'Areee... This traffic is a problem in these cities. Every person is in a hurry. Nobody wants to let the other go first. 'said Peter in an irritated manner. 'Hmm...' The taxi driver replied uninterested. 'Blast in Aurora. Blast in Aurora.' A man running towards the traffic shouted. 'Time bomb was fitted in one chair' said another. The whole situation looked like as a sense of sorrow hit them. Peter couldn't believe what he was hearing. He rang Jennifer. Not reachable. He rang again, not reachable. No difference in the third. His mind started to get blocked. Tears started to roll. He could sense the driver asking him something but couldn't hear it. Panic had taken over him. He started to feel dizzy. But he gathered himself quickly and came out of the car, Started running rather trembling through the traffic.

A few minutes later he went dark. (Next day) 'Please come' said the policeman. 'Are they your wife and kid?' asked the policeman while writing down his notes. Peter didn't say anything. Yes it was Jennifer and Chris. But tears didn't roll out his eyes now. He stood rock still staring blankly at the bodies, without blinking. Suddenly he heard Jennifer's voice, 'You are late Peter, you are too late' Peter stood in front of the gravestone of Jennifer and Chris. He laid the rose near Jennifer, sat near them, and took out a box full of sandwiches. 'Look Chris I brought your favorite sandwich. But it's not as good as your mamma's. You know how I cook' 'Jenny my work is going well. There's a lot of work pending for this week but I'll manage it. And there's good news too. I might soon get a promotion. Yes, you always had wished for this. 'Suddenly Peter's smile faded away. He stopped talking. A chilly wind went past. A drop of tear came out but he quickly wiped it off. After a pause, he said 'You and Chris left me all alone. Wish I would have been on time that day. At least we could be together now. 'He stood up and started to leave. He reached near the gate and heard a man running 'Blast at Hotel Pristine, big blast'. A man hurried out of the taxi crying and ran through the traffic. Peter stared at the whole situation. Took out his phone and set the message for Sunday morning. He looked back, and smiled 'See you again this Sunday, and I promise I won't be late. Goodbye'.

Urmila Chakraborty

The writer is a passionate writer apart from being a research scholar in Chemistry. She has been writing poems and short stories in Hindi and English since the age of 8. She has participated in many national-level writing competitions.

The Diamond Explorers

There were two men, both were diamond explorers. Though they were from different countries, they came across each other while searching for a precious and beautiful diamond, which they had heard of in old tales, but none had ever seen. They got together to explore the diamond and searched many places over years. They wandered across the globe, and went to all possible areas where the precious diamond could be found. Many times they even risked their lives, and even got cheated by the people who gave them false guidance regarding the whereabouts of the gem. But they could never find a diamond similar to the description of the tales. Eventually, they both became friends. One of them was very rational and believed in his mind and sense of judgement more than anything else. He was just focused on finding the diamond. The second one believed his heart and was always full of hope. He enjoyed his explorations, and was always grateful about whatever experiences he had throughout his journey. Now many years passed and both of them thought of giving up quite unwillingly. They had dreamt day and night about finding the diamond, put so many years of hard work, it had almost become the main purpose of their life. Finally they decided to return to their respective countries and do something else. On the day when they had to part ways, they thought of relaxing by taking a walk on a secluded beach. While they were walking, a thing shining dimly in the sand caught the attention of the first friend.

The second friend was little behind him so he did not see the thing at first. The first friend's heart told him to dig up the thing, but his mind told him that it was a mere shell or a piece of glass, so he moved ahead. Now the second one reached that point and saw the shiny thing. He dug it out of the sand, and to his surprise, it was a stone quite similar to the shape and size of the described diamond but not as bright or beautiful as it. He went to the first one to show that to him, but the first friend was least interested and told him that their luck was just playing games, after putting so much effort for a precious diamond, what they finally found was a similar looking ordinary stone. But the second friend thought of keeping it as a memoir of his explorations. He thought that even if it was not a real diamond, it would be a beautiful stone if cleaned, so he kept it as a final gift of God. On reaching home, he took off the dirt and algal growth that had covered the stone over years. To his astonishment, he found a bright and beautiful diamond, which might have been among the treasures of any ship, wrecked long ago and might have been buried in the sand over years and resurfaced to be found by the second friend. God fulfills our wishes sooner or later but his plans and timings may differ from our expectations...The one with hope, faith and positive attitude can realise his blessings on time.

Saving the dog

It was a calm beautiful Sunday morning. Everything was perfectly calm. Me and my elder sister had our breakfast and went on the terrace to observe the surroundings. The breeze was blowing and the trees were swaying. The chirping of birds made everything more pleasant. We were strolling and having a conversation. Suddenly the tranquility was interrupted by barking sound of several dogs. Firstly we thought that the street dogs were just having regular petty fights or just barking and running after some random animal or car. But the noise was very disturbing. So we hurried at the corner of the terrace to have a look of what was going on. The sight was very unusual. A ferocious Pitbull terrier escaped from someone's house and was causing all the havoc. 9-10 street dogs got scared of that single dog and were barking at it from a distance. But it was running like a mad animal and started chasing the street dogs. For the first time I saw so many street dogs getting so timid in front of a small looking dog. All the street dogs were running away from the pitbull to save themselves as it was too energetic and scary. But the pitbull caught hold of one unfortunate dog, twice its size. It just grabbed the street dog with its sharp teeth and looked as if it was going to tear him apart. All the other dogs were trying to save it but from a distance because they were afraid for their own lives. The dog was trying hard to escape but the pitbull showed no mercy. Luckily it could loosen the grip of the Pitbull's teeth and slide away.

It was not able to run but tried as hard as he could. The pitbull again pounced to grab it. But the street dog managed to go to a nearby shanty. A family lived there with four kids who were also watching all this turmoil. The pitbull got distracted for a while and tried to chase other dogs. Following their wit, the kids came out of their shanty and quickly hid the injured street dog under a pile of straws kept near their small hut, and covered it with a big black polythene sheet. Unable to catch another street dog, the pit bull came near the shanty to search for the injured dog. It was unable to find the injured dog but started sniffing its smell and approaching the covered straw stack. My heart was pounding with fear of what might happen next. But fortunately, the owners of the pitbull arrived. They tamed their ferocious beast and took it away. Everything was calm again. The loud barks ceased. Other tired street dogs dispersed. I was worried about the injured dog. But the brave kids came out of their shanty and took off the plastic sheet. The dog was weak, still unable to walk. The kids adored it, and encouraged it to get up. But it tried and fell down. Then the kids gave it some water to drink, then poured water over its body. Firstly I thought that was not good but my mother said they are doing the correct thing as it would help the self-healing of the dog. Slowly the dog got strength. After about an hour it got up again. It was wagging its tail to thank the little kids, who started playing with the dog happily. We all were relieved to.

The Wordings

"Reviving literature in the era of technology."

Publish your solo book with us.

20% discount on all our packages for co-authors of the anthology.

Join our project

#MakeIndiaWrite

Contact:

Instagram: @thewordings1

Email: contact@thewordings.com

Web: www.thewordings.com

www.ingramcontent.com/pod-product-compliance
Lightning Source LLC
Chambersburg PA
CBHW052258150726
48001CB00024B/2033